Copyrighted Material

The King and the Monster: Let's Talk About Addiction

Copyright © 2023 by Kathleen Lockwood. All Rights Reserved.

No part of this publication may be reproduced, stored in a retrieval system or transmitted, in any form or by any means—electronic, mechanical, photocopying, recording or otherwise—without prior written permission from the publisher, except for the inclusion of brief quotations in a review.

For information about this title or to order other books and/or electronic media, contact the publisher:

Kathleen Lockwood/Diotima Press
BooksbyKathi.com
Kathi@booksbykathi.com

ISBNs:
978-0-9642128-7-9 (hardcover)
978-0-9642128-8-6 (softcover)
978-0-9642128-9-3 (eBook)

Printed in the United States of America

Cover and Interior design: 1106 Design

Foreword

As a mental health therapist and addiction counselor for the past twenty years, I've known many families that have been affected by substance abuse.

Unfortunately, addiction is not just an individual problem; it permeates the entire family system. As adults face their own fears, anger, and sadness, it can be a struggle to give children an understanding about what's happening. Children and their voices are often overlooked as the chaos of addiction ensues.

Kathi Lockwood, an interfaith minister and accomplished author, has written a profound and powerful story that strikes at the heart of addiction as a family disease.

She artfully uses storytelling to begin the challenging conversations that need to be had when addiction causes the physical removal or emotional distance of a family member. The imagery of pain and healing throughout the story helps children understand and develop empathy for the king and why the monster takes hold.

The King and the Monster allows children to identify their complicated and confusing feelings and assures them that the changes happening around them are not their fault.

It is sometimes very difficult to see that a happy ending is possible. *The King and the Monster* teaches us that asking for help can begin a process of healing and connectedness that will shield us from the monsters in our world. Through family, community, and his angels, the king and his family find a way to be whole again.

This storybook should be on the shelf of every addiction therapist, school counselor, and public library. I hope for the sake of families struggling with addiction that this story reaches their hands and begins a process of healing that dark spot in their hearts.

—Chelsea Markopoulos, MA, CAADC, LPC

Chelsea Markopoulos began her career as an outpatient counselor for adolescents with substance abuse issues. Later, as a clinical coordinator, she continued to provide therapy for adults and adolescents in an outpatient addictions program. She has been in private practice since 2010.

Introduction

"The possibility of renewal exists so long as life exists. How to support that possibility in others and in ourselves is the ultimate question."

—Gabor Maté, *In the Realm of Hungry Ghosts: Close Encounters with Addiction*

This book began with a phone call.

When I answered that call, I heard the desperate voice of a beloved family member.

"Robbie* just went into rehab, and now Annie* doesn't know why her daddy had to move away. Can you write a book that will help me explain this to her?"

Instinctively, I said yes, but then I immediately thought, "How am I going to do that?" Addiction is a disease that is so painful and so complex. How would I be able to explain all that to a five year old?

"I'll figure it out," I told myself.

I am an interfaith minister and the author of two children's books, but I did not expect this "assignment." However, with the full understanding of the pain that affects the family of an addict, I was aware of how important, and healing, a paradigm-shifting story would be.

A few days later, I found myself on a very late flight to the West Coast with my three-year-old granddaughter sound asleep with her head on my lap.

With hours to go and my earbuds in, I closed my eyes, happy that I could finally meditate. It had been a hectic day traveling with my daughter and her two little girls, especially with a six-hour delay. Now, I finally had some peace! It did not last very long, though, for almost immediately after closing my eyes, this book revealed itself.

In my mind's eye, it progressed: the title, the story, the visuals. Upon its completion, I immediately pulled out my laptop and in the quiet darkness at 30,000 feet, I began to write. With arms outstretched to the tray table next to me, I recorded my first quick draft. *The King and the Monster* was born.

*names have been changed

About This Book

The imagery used in this story is designed to inspire your child's questions. The depth of your heart-to-heart conversation will be determined by the child's age, experience, and level of understanding.

Dr. Gabor Maté, a well-known author, physician, and expert on addiction and mental illness, describes trauma as an unfillable hole in the heart, and the root cause of addiction. Additionally, the scars of trauma are often inherited, and are multigenerational.

In this story, the "shadow of sadness" is the language I use to describe trauma. Throughout the book, I make it clear that the king's shadow came from "long ago," and that it shrank when his children were born. This is an important concept because children will frequently blame themselves for their parent's problems, and this perspective can help alleviate this concern.

I also include the concept of a "Higher Power," which comes directly from the Alcoholics Anonymous (AA) manual. A Higher Power could be thought of as God, your Higher Self, or the Universe. In the simplest terms, it is a power greater than oneself and one's personal share of Infinite Life. Your own spiritual beliefs will serve you here.

Not every story of addiction has a happy ending, but this one does. The possibility of health and healing exists so long as there is life. *The King and the Monster* was written to support that possibility and to touch our struggling hearts with peace as we share the joy of a happy ending with the King and his family.

I hope you find the book engaging and inspiring, and that it helps initiate a deep and healing conversation with your loved ones about the complex illness of addiction.

Once upon a time, there was a very happy King, and he had a very happy family.

The King loved his royal Queen.

He loved his beautiful children.

He even loved his spunky little dog.

Some nights, after dinner, they would all eat ice cream together. He loved that.

And when his children went to bed, he would read to them. He loved that, too!

The King had a beautiful heart, but, inside it, there was a shadow of sadness that had been there a long, long time. When his children were born, the shadow shrank, but it still lingered.

In his kingdom, there was a Wisdom Tree, where the villagers gathered and played together. The King's team of Guardian Angels loved to watch him play with his family there.

There was also a deep quicksand pit in his kingdom. The wise grandparents told the villagers never to go to such a dangerous place.

One day, the King's friends invited him to play at the quicksand pit.

"No, no, no," said the King. "It is dangerous there."

"Come on," they said. "It will be fun."

The King was curious about the fun he might have at the pit.

It's probably not so dangerous, he thought. Maybe it will help the shadow in my heart go away.

"Besides," he declared, "I am a King! I am smart and strong. Nothing bad can happen to me."

So, the King ignored his Guardian Angels' signs and explored the quicksand pit with his friends.

He put his hand in it. "See? I'm fine!" he said. "This isn't dangerous."

But it was a trap! At that very moment, the Monster grabbed him.

At first, the Monster pretended to be his friend.

But then, silently, the Monster grew strong and made the King very sick. The King's sickness made him do things he did not want to do!

Now, sometimes, the King behaved just like a Monster!

He roared at his royal Queen, *but he didn't want to.*

He yelled at his beautiful children, *but he didn't want to.*

He even barked at his spunky little dog, *but he didn't want to.*

The King was sick, and everyone was very UN-happy!

The King was so weak that the Monster easily dragged him back to the deep quicksand pit. The King was frightened and lonely.

"I miss my happy life! I want my family back!" he cried. "I love my Queen! I love my children! Somebody, please help me get away from this Monster!"

Just then, his Guardian Angels sent a beam of light to him. This made the Monster growl, but it gave the King a good idea! "I know! I'll ask the village Wisdom Tree!"

"Wisdom Tree, I want to be healthy again. I love my family! I want my happy life back. How do I rid myself of this Monster?"

The tree smiled and gently embraced him. The tree said, "Now that you've asked, the village Healing Helpers are on their way to take you to the Healing House!"

The king did not want to move away from his family, but he knew he needed help to get better and be happy again. Bravely, he followed the Healing Helpers to the Healing House.

The Healing Helpers told him they had all fought off the Monster before and won! So, he could, too!

The Healing Helpers knew how to make good decisions to avoid the Monster. They would teach the King how to get rid of the Monster, too!

The next day was the King's daughter's birthday. But the Princess was very sad.

"Where is my daddy?" she cried. "Why isn't he here?"

The Queen was sad, too. "Honey," she said, "your daddy wants to be with us now, but he is very sick. He is in a special school to learn how to be healthy again. He will come home as soon as he can."

"Okay," the princess sighed. "I can wait."

The following day, the King's son started throwing his toys around. "I am so angry!" the Prince yelled. "I want my daddy!"

The Queen hugged him. "I understand. We all feel a little angry! We miss your daddy very much. Just remember that he is getting the help he needs to be healthy and happy again." The Prince hugged his mother. "I can wait," he whispered.

The King's family visited him at the Healing House. They were happy to see that he loved them more than ever!

The Healing Helpers reminded the King that he was not alone and that a Higher Power could help him conquer the Monster. They taught him to listen to his angels—*and he became wiser.*

The Healing Helpers reminded him of his bold and beautiful heart. They helped him heal the shadow of sadness in his heart—*and he became more loving.*

They reminded him of his inner courage and strength—*and he became more powerful.*

The Healing Helpers gave the King armor and tools to protect himself from any other Monsters. They taught him how to use his wisdom, love, and power to make good decisions, so that he would never fall into the Monster's trap again.

Every day, he got stronger, and the Monster got weaker, until, finally, the Monster disappeared.

The King was free to go home!

His family was so happy to have their daddy back!

The King kissed the royal Queen.

The King kissed his beautiful children.

He even kissed his spunky little dog!

The King was so happy to eat ice cream with his family again!

Every night, he put his head on his favorite pillow and thanked all the Guardian Angels and Healing Helpers who had helped him to be healthy and happy again!

Acknowledgements

There are many to whom I owe my thanks for assisting me in bringing this book to fruition.

Many thanks to my children, Trieste, Dominick, and Amelia, who I love beyond measure. Your input and advice supported me from the very beginning.

I offer a very singular thank you to E.H. Without your phone call on that fateful night, this book might not exist. May love and health continue to bless your family.

I send my blessings, love, and infinite gratitude to you, Matt Neptune, my real-life Healing Helper, and superhero. Thanks to you and all the Healing Helpers who devote their lives to saving lives.

Uniquely, I greatly appreciate Joyce Eisenberg, my treasured friend, and invaluable editor. You helped me smooth out my rough draft and then some! Your friendship is a blessing to me.

Thank you, Sam Horn, author extraordinaire—your words of wisdom and encouragement continue to light my way.

Many friends and acquaintances read my early drafts, listened to my storytelling, and contributed with insightful comments and questions. I am so grateful to all of you!

Many thanks to Jill Howell, ATR-BC, LPC, Frank Kepner, Mark Lichty, Crystal Kelly, John Knowles, MA, CADC, Linnea Pond, Tarah Probst, Andrea Rimburg, Christine Schmeider, Mariellen Smith, Jack and Jill Swerzie, and Skip Scheetz.

To the members of my Oasis group, thank you for your shared wisdom, friendship, and encouragement that supported and guided me on this venture.

I'd also like to thank Chelsea Markopoulos, MA, CAADC, LPC, and Mary Pat Melvin, LSW, CDAC, MS. You inspired me with your comments on this story's therapeutic value.

My heart goes out to all individuals and families struggling with this dreadful disease and to those who have suffered a loss. May peace and love enter our hearts, and together with love, may we heal.

About the Author

Kathi Lockwood, M.Ed., is an Interfaith Minister, Reiki Master and spiritual optimist. She is the founder and CEO of the Heart Self Speaks Collective, a virtual home for those on spiritual journeys.

In addition to *The King and the Monster,* she is the author of *An Adoption Made in Heaven: Amy Angel Goes Home,* a paradigm-shifting story informing children that their journey to their parents was divinely guided, and *A Christmas Eve Adventure: Finding the Light of the World,* an interfaith narrative illustrating that we all carry the light.

You can find her in the Pocono Mountains writing, meditating or sipping coffee with her poodle Monet at her side.

Kathi Lockwood is available for speaking engagements, podcasts, and book clubs, and can be contacted at *Kathi@booksbykathi.com.*

About the Artists

Ade Chintya is an Indonesian-based illustrator and member of the society of children's Book Writers and Illustrators. For more information, please visit www.adechint.com.

Puteri Delphia Esther is an Art Director based in Indonesia, specializing in Illustration. For more information, please visit www.puteriesther.com.

Made in the USA
Coppell, TX
15 March 2024